Jack Be Nimble

Jack, be nimble.
Jack, be quick.
Jack, jump over
the candlestick.

Jack jumped high.
Jack jumped low.
Jack jumped over
and burned his toe.

adapted by Jeffrey B. Fuerst • illustrated by Garry Colby

Jack runs and jumps.

"Are you ready?" asks the coach.

"I am ready," says Jack.

"On your mark. Get set. Go," says the coach.

"Go, Jack, go," say the fans.

Jack runs fast.

Jack runs very fast.

Jack jumps high.

Jack jumps very high.

"Jump, Jack, jump," say the fans.

Jack jumps over the candlestick!